"TOO SMART" JONES

and the
Dangerous
Woman

Get swept away in the many Gilbert Morris Adventures available from Moody Press:

"Too Smart" Jones Series

Join Juliet "Too Smart" Jones and her home schooled friends as they attempt to solve exciting mysteries. Active Series for ages 7-12.

Dixie Morris Animal Adventures

Follow the exciting adventures of this animal lover as she learns more of God and His character through her many adventures underneath the Big Top. Ten Book Series for ages 7-12.

The Daystar Voyages

Join the crew of the Daystar as they traverse the wide expanse of space. Adventure and danger abound, but they learn time and again that God is truly the Master of the Universe. Active Series for ages 10-14.

Bonnets and Bugles Series

Follow good friends Leah Carter and Jeff Majors as they experience danger, intrigue, compassion, and love in these civil war adventures. Ten Book Series for ages 10-14.

The Seven Sleepers Series

Go with Josh and his friends as they are sent by Goél, their spiritual leader, on dangerous and challenging voyages to conquer the forces of darkness in the new world. Ten Book Series for ages 10-14. Watch for the new Lost Chronicles of the Seven Sleepers!

4

A GILBERT MORRIS MYSTERY

MOODY PRESS
CHICAGO

Moody Press, a ministry of the
Moody Bible Institute, is designed for education,
evangelization, and edification. If we may assist you
in knowing more about Christ and the Christian
life, please write us without obligation:
Moody Press, c/o MLM, Chicago, IL 60610.

ISBN: 0-8024-4028-2

1 3 5 7 9 10 8 6 4 2

Printed in the United States of America

Contents

1. The Woman in the Alley   7
2. A New Project   17
3. Dumpster Queen   27
4. Juliet's Scare   35
5. Ducks   45
6. Juliet Is Caught   53
7. More Detective Work   61
8. Trouble for Juliet   69
9. Butcher Knife Annie   81
10. A Giant Step   87
11. Butcher Knife Annie's Story   97
12. The New Annie   103

1

The Woman in the Alley

"Joe, will you hurry up and *move!*"

Joe Jones looked up at his sister and frowned impatiently. "I've got to think about this move," he said.

He was sitting cross-legged across from Juliet in the back of the family van. The checkerboard was between them. Joe's men were red. He only had three left. Juliet had eight. It was a hopeless situation.

But Joe Jones was probably the most stubborn nine-year-old in the United States of America. Even when he got down to one man and his sister had ten or twelve left, he wouldn't give up. Not until the last move was made.

Juliet sighed and leaned back against the side of the car. "I don't see why you're wasting time. You can't *possibly* win, Joe."

"You don't know what I could do. A miracle

could happen. Why, you could lose your memory." Then Joe glared at his older sister. She was ten. "I don't think you know as much as you think you know, Too Smart Jones."

"Well, I think I know I'm going to win this checker game!" Juliet snapped. "I can't even *remember* the last time you won. I don't know why you want to play checkers, anyway."

"Juliet, stop tormenting your brother." Mr. Jones turned his eyes away from the road ahead just long enough to glance back at them. He was a redheaded man with blue eyes, and right then there was a frown on his forehead. "Joe is right. You may be Too Smart Jones to some people, but you don't need to brag about it."

"Dad, I wasn't bragging about anything!" Juliet pouted. "And I *hate* that name Too Smart Jones! Tell him, Mom. Tell him how much I hate it."

Her mother reached back and patted Juliet on the knee. "I know you do, honey," she said. She turned to Juliet's dad. "Don't fuss at her. She really can't help it if the kids call her names. You know how kids are about things like that."

"That's right, Daddy," Juliet said. "You know how skinny Matilda Simmons is. Well, some of the kids call her Bird Legs."

"Well, that's a very cruel thing to do. And I hope you'll never be guilty of doing anything like that." Mrs. Jones turned back to looking at the road. "Now, finish your checker game. We're almost there."

At that exact moment, the car hit a pothole. The bump threw Juliet forward against Joe. She knocked all the checkers off the board.

"Get off of me!" Joe grunted. "You weigh a ton!"

"I couldn't help it. It was that old bump in the road."

"Well, the game's over now," Joe said with satisfaction. "I could have won, too."

"No, it's not over. I can put those checkers back right where they were."

"I wouldn't trust you." He grinned at her. "You've probably forgotten how many I had. Six, wasn't it?"

"It was not six!"

Joe laughed and crawled forward on his knees to lean over the front seat. "Dad," he said, "when are we going to get rid of this piece of junk?"

"What piece of junk?" Mr. Jones glared at his son in the rearview mirror. "I'll have you know this is a fine car."

"Aw, Dad, why don't we get a *real* car?"

"This *is* a real car. It's a Chevrolet van, and it's only eight years old."

"Eight years old! Then, you've had this thing since—" Joe did some subtraction in his head "—since I was one year old. That's too long to keep a car," he said importantly. "You ought to get a new car at least every other year. And it ought to be a good one."

"What kind would you suggest—and where do you think I'd get the money for a 'good one'?"

"Why, you've got lots of money in the bank. I saw you did yesterday when Mom was paying bills."

"You can stop prying into my bank account. And I'll have no more rude remarks about this car. It's got only ninety-two thousand miles on it. It's good for another ten years."

Joe said, "You mean I've got to ride in this thing until I graduate from high school?"

Juliet laughed. "It's a good enough car for you. Besides, I like this car. Of course," she added, "when I get to be sixteen and have my own car, it won't be like this one."

"When I get to be sixteen, I'll get a car, too." Joe leaned forward again and put a hand on his dad's shoulder. "I know exactly what kind of car I want, Dad. A fire-engine-red Viper!"

"A viper! That's a snake!" Juliet protested.

"That's what you think! It's a sports car. Why, it'll go from zero to a hundred miles an hour in five seconds."

"And where would you drive it?" Juliet asked. "On a race track?"

"You can both stop arguing, because nobody's going to get a Viper. I remember when you could buy a pretty nice house for the money it would take to buy that car!"

"Aw, Dad, you remember when you could buy a Coke for a nickel, too."

They were coming to Oakwood's main business section. Since it was Saturday, it could be hard to find a place to park. "I'd better park here," Mr. Jones said. "We'll have to walk the rest of the way."

Juliet's dad parked the van near an alley that cut between two buildings. They all got out.

"What's *she* doing?" Joe asked at once.

Juliet looked into the alley and saw a strange figure. It was a woman pulling an old red wagon behind her. The wagon was filled with what looked like junk. On top were some heads of lettuce that she was taking from a green dumpster behind the supermarket.

"I've never seen *her* before. She looks weird!" Juliet said.

"Be quiet, Juliet! She'll hear you!" her mother said.

But Juliet was fascinated by the woman. Now she was leaning into the dumpster, digging out something else. She brought up a bunch of limp carrots and tossed it onto the red wagon.

And then the woman turned her head. She stared up the alley at the Jones family, and Juliet got a good look at her. She was very tall, and her hair was mostly gray. She had a long nose and thin lips. Her face was wrinkled, and her clothes were almost like a Halloween costume. She was skinny and stooped over. And since she wore a long, faded brown dress that came down to her ankles, she did look something like a witch. Her shoes were men's working shoes without shoestrings.

"Well, what you staring at?"

The woman's voice creaked like a door that had not been used much.

"She's got a knife!" Joe said.

The woman did, indeed, have a knife hanging from a belt around her skinny waist. She jerked it out and waved it. "It's to cut the noses off of kids like you!" she said.

"Let's go," Mr. Jones said firmly. He seemed embarrassed by his children, and he practically hauled them past the alley.

"I can't believe you two were so impolite and rude!" their mother scolded.

"I didn't say anything," Joe said, "except that she had a knife."

"You two stood staring at her as if she was some kind of a freak," Mr. Jones said. "I thought we'd taught you better than that."

Juliet did not like for her father to fuss at her. "I didn't say a word," she said quickly.

"Yes, you did, and you stared at her," Mrs. Jones said. "She's a very unfortunate woman. Anybody can see that."

"Now I know who she is," Mr. Jones said suddenly. "Dave Stevens told me about her."

Dave Stevens owned the big supermarket where the Joneses bought most of their groceries. "She came to town not long ago. Everybody's been calling her Butcher Knife Annie because of that big knife she carries around."

"She certainly looks like she needs help," Mrs. Jones said as they walked along. "Does she have any family?"

"Dave didn't say. And I'm not sure that anybody knows."

"Where does she live?"

"In a one-room shack over by the railroad. It's down in Shanty Town."

Mrs. Jones frowned. "It seems there ought to be *some* government office that can help a woman like that. Or some charity organization."

"With that knife, I bet she'd cut anybody's throat who tried to get close to her," Juliet said.

"Why, Juliet, I'm ashamed of you! Here's this poor woman who has nothing, and you're making fun of her!"

Juliet opened her mouth to defend herself. But she could think of nothing to say.

"You're a bright girl, Juliet!" her father went on. "But it's more important to be kind than to be bright."

"That's right," Mrs. Jones agreed. "It's kindness that counts more in this world."

The rest of the trip into town was not fun for Juliet. Her parents' criticism stung—especially because she knew they were right. And she said almost nothing on the way home.

Joe whispered so that their mother and father could not hear. "She *was* a crazy looking old woman, wasn't she? She looked kind of like a witch. She won't have to get dressed up for Halloween. She's all ready for it."

"Don't talk about her, Joe!"

Joe stared at Juliet, then laughed. "Well, look who's teaching me good manners. I don't notice you've got any medals for being kind, Too Smart. Maybe they'll be calling you Too Rude Jones."

Juliet ordinarily would have flared up at Joe. But this time she didn't answer. Indeed, she felt terrible. She knew that she would feel that way for a long time.

After Juliet and Joe helped unload the groceries, Juliet left the house and went for a walk down the street. She had not gone far before she ran into Chili Williams.

Chili, whose real name was Roy, was nine years old. He was an African-American boy with large ears that stuck out from his head. He had on a crimson T-shirt, some cutoff jeans, and a pair of worn Nikes. "Hey, how you doing, Juliet?"

"OK."

Chili looked at her more closely and frowned. "What's the matter with you?" he asked. "You don't look OK to me."

For a moment Juliet hesitated. But she had always found Chili a good person to talk to when she had a problem. "I just did something that wasn't nice, Chili," she said slowly.

"What was it?"

He listened as Juliet told about her experience with the old woman in the alley.

"Oh yeah! I know about her. Everybody calls her Butcher Knife Annie. She's been in town about a month, I guess."

"Did you ever talk to her?"

"Me? Not me. I started to once, but she just frowned at me. Man, she's got a face that's like sour milk!"

"Well, I know I didn't treat her right, Chili, and I'm sorry about it."

"A lot of the kids make fun of her. The way she looks and where she lives. You're not the only one."

"Do you know where she lives?"

"Oh yeah. It's a little one-room shack. Doesn't even have an inside bathroom."

At that moment Joe came along on his bicycle. He wheeled to a stop. "What are you two talking about?"

"About Butcher Knife Annie," Chili answered.

"She's probably wanted by the police someplace."

"Joe! You don't know anything about it."

"Well, I know she needs a bath. Doesn't take a genius to know that, Too Smart Jones."

"If you can't say anything nice about her, don't say anything at all, Joe!"

Chili pulled a baseball out of his hip pocket and tossed it in the air. He gave both Juliet and Joe a sideways look, then said, "I've had some pretty bad things said about me too. And I can tell you right now it's no fun." He turned around and walked off, leaving them looking after him.

Her brother balanced on his bicycle for a moment. He said, "You'd better stay away from that Butcher Knife Annie, Juliet. I think she might be crazy." Then he pedaled away at full speed.

Juliet said good-bye to Chili and continued to walk slowly along the sidewalk. *I wonder why she lives the way she does?* she thought. *She wasn't always dirty. And she didn't always live in a shack, I'll bet.* She walked even more slowly, thinking. Then she said out loud, "I bet I could find out more about her if I just wanted to. Why, I bet there's even a kind of mystery about her."

And Juliet Jones decided then and there, "I *am* going to find out more about Butcher Knife Annie—you wait and see if I don't!"

2

A New Project

The extra upstairs bedroom that Joe and Juliet Jones used as a schoolroom was an attractive place. Their mother had put up pretty blue curtains and found some throw rugs to match. But the room was cluttered. Both Juliet and Joe tended to be pack rats. Neither of them ever threw anything away unless they were ordered to do so.

An old poster showing the Jones family tree hung on one wall. Another poster was a leaf display. Still another was of glittering silver stars mounted on dark blue. On a table in the corner sat a large clay volcano with some gooey red lava running over its side. A popsicle skyscraper towered on the corner of Joe's desk.

Suddenly Juliet looked up from the book she was reading and said, "I think we need a new project."

"What kind of a project?"

"I don't know. But something different."

"How about we do a study of monster movies? That way we could get Mom to check us out *The Wolf Man* and *Frankenstein* and *The Mummy*. And all the good old scary movies."

"I don't think Mom would ever go for that," Juliet said. "Maybe we could do a study of *Gone with the Wind.*"

"Yuck! I don't want to see that thing ever again!"

"It's the best movie ever made," Juliet said. "Oh, I just love it when Scarlett comes down that curling staircase."

They argued back and forth. Then suddenly Juliet cried, "I've got a *good* idea, Joe!"

"You have about thirty good ideas a day— with gusts up to fifty! What is it this time?"

"No. This one is really good. Listen. Why don't we do a study on homeless people?"

"You mean people that rent their houses instead of owning them?"

"No, no! I mean people who don't have anyplace to live."

Joe picked up his model of a jet aircraft. It was a Navy Tomcat, and he had spent many weeks getting it just right. He zoomed it through the air, making the movements of a jet plane. Finally he set it down and shook his head. "Naw. I don't think there are enough homeless people around here to investigate.

You have to be in a big city to have a lot of homeless people."

"Well, maybe we could just investigate poor people, then."

Joe gave Juliet a hard glance. "I know what you're up to, Too Smart Jones!"

"I'm not up to anything."

"Yes, you are too! You're wanting to investigate Butcher Knife Annie, that's what. I'll bet you think there's some kind of a mystery about her, don't you? Maybe you think she's a fairy princess."

"Oh, that's silly, Joe!"

"No sillier than some of the other investigations you've gotten me into."

Juliet opened the blue cookie jar on her desk and took out an M&M. She put it into her mouth and chewed it, thinking.

Joe said, "You know what Mom says about eating those before dinner."

"I'm only eating one."

"Well, give me one, then. Or maybe you owe me three. I saw you eat those other two."

They sat and argued about that. After a while they evened out the number of M&Ms that each had eaten.

Then Joe said importantly, "I think homeless people are that way because they want to be."

"What are you talking about? They're poor!"

"Their own fault. There's plenty of jobs around. They're all lazy!"

"Joe, that's mean! You shouldn't talk like that!"

And then Juliet began tapping her chin with her forefinger. Joe scowled. He probably hated to see this, for it meant that his sister was *thinking!* And when Juliet Jones *thought*, that meant that she had some idea in mind. And when Juliet had an idea, Joe usually found himself caught up in it.

Just as Juliet was about to speak, the door opened, and their mother came in. "Why don't you two go outside and take a break? I could hear you arguing all the way downstairs."

"Well, Juliet's had a dumb idea again," Joe said.

"Really? A dumb idea?" Mrs. Jones looked at her daughter and smiled. "Well, it wouldn't be the first dumb idea you've had."

"Mom, don't say that! You know my ideas are pretty good—sometimes."

"So what is this big idea?"

"I just thought it might be a good project to do a study of homeless people."

"Where did you get that idea?"

"It's that Butcher Knife Annie, that's where. Juliet thinks Butcher Knife Annie's got some sort of secret. You know—like Spiderman."

"She's not like Spiderman at all!"

"Oh, you know what I mean. Spiderman

wears a mask and all. And nobody knows who he is. And Superman pretends to be Clark Kent." Joe grinned. "And people must be pretty blind, because when he puts his glasses on they don't recognize he's really Superman with glasses on.

"Anyway," Joe finished, "that's what Juliet's up to, Mom. She's into another one of her famous 'cases.'"

"I'm sure Annie is just an unfortunate woman," Mrs. Jones said firmly. "Don't you be bothering her, now. Either of you."

Juliet did not answer. Instead, she jumped up and began to pull on her coat. Then she grabbed a toboggan hat and pulled it down over her ears. "Come on, Joe. Let's take a break and go outside, like Mom says."

Joe got a heavy sweatshirt and followed Juliet out the front door. As soon as they were outside, he said, "Race you!" He took off at once, running as hard as he could.

Juliet called after him, "I don't want to race. And I'm going over to Jenny's house."

Joe hollered something back, but Juliet could not understand him. She ambled down the street, admiring the fall leaves. They had turned orange, yellow, red, and gold. They made a beautiful sight. She knew soon they would all fall, and then the trees would be bare and not so pretty. Now, however, she enjoyed the colors as she walked along toward Jenny's house.

Jenny White had become a very close friend. She was one year younger than Juliet, but the two enjoyed doing things together.

Jenny opened the door as soon as Juliet knocked. "Come on in," she said. "I'm making popcorn."

"Sounds good to me."

Soon the two of them were propped in front of the television, eating popcorn and drinking hot chocolate out of thick mugs.

Jenny's mother came in after a while. She smiled at them. "What are you two plotting?" she asked. "I'm always afraid when you get together."

"Why, Mom, we don't ever do anything bad!" Jenny protested. Her blue eyes sparkled.

"That's right. We're good girls, Mrs. White," Juliet said. "Sugar and spice and everything nice. That's what we're made of."

Mrs. White laughed at them. "You two don't get into any kind of mischief. Oh, no. Never."

As her mother turned to leave the room, Jenny said, "Mom, we're going out for a while. All right?"

"All right, but be sure you put on a coat."

The two girls strolled along the streets of Oakwood. They talked awhile about their studies. And then Juliet brought up the subject of Butcher Knife Annie and other homeless people.

But Jenny suddenly turned pale. She stopped abruptly on the sidewalk and stared hard at Juliet. "Don't you have anything to do with her!" she warned.

"Why, Jenny, what's wrong with you?"

"I'm afraid of her."

"But—she's harmless enough."

"You don't know that. She carries around that big butcher knife. And who knows what she's done where she used to live."

Juliet knew that Jenny was a timid girl. She was always afraid of anything new. But Juliet also was impatient. "Look," she said. "Joe and I have been talking about doing a school project on poor people. I thought you would want to do it with us."

Juliet argued for a long time, but she couldn't change Jenny's mind.

Jenny said, "Juliet, I want you to promise me to just stay away from that woman. It's for your own good."

Finally Juliet said crossly, "Oh, all right! If that's the way you feel about it!"

What Jenny did not know was that Juliet had her fingers crossed behind her back. More than once Juliet had heard her father say, "Crossing your fingers doesn't have anything to do with telling the truth." This time, however, Juliet thought she was in the right. *If it will make Jenny feel better, then let her think I won't go to see Butcher Knife Annie.*

When they came to the square in Oakwood, there was Joe, sitting on a bench. He was watching some old men play checkers.

The girls said hi and were about to move on past when Juliet happened to hear somebody say, "Butcher Knife Annie." She grabbed Jenny's arm. "Wait, Jenny! Wait a minute! Let's hear what they're saying."

One of the checker players was talking. "And so I'm saying that old woman is crazy."

"She's a danger to the community the way she carries that knife around! That's what she is," another player said.

The first man nodded wisely. "The chief wanted to make her leave town. But he says there's no law to keep her from being here."

"He's got a badge, hasn't he? He's got a gun. He ought to run her out of town today before she hurts somebody."

"Well, he tried. But she didn't pay no attention to the chief."

"You know what I heard? I heard that some folks are getting up a petition."

"What kind of petition?"

"To get her put in a mental hospital and get her off the streets."

Juliet gasped when she heard this.

Jenny tugged at her arm. She was looking at Juliet with a strange expression on her face.

"You promised, Juliet!" Jenny whispered. "You promised. Now *please* stay away from Butcher Knife Annie. I don't want you to get hurt."

Juliet felt sorry for Jenny, who was so afraid of everything. And she felt pleased with herself. *She* wasn't afraid. She said, "Don't you worry about me. I'll be all right."

But she was still thinking, *I'm going to find out who Butcher Knife Annie is. And what she's doing here. And why she looks so sad. And then I'm going to find out why she lives the way she does. There's got to be some reason, and I'm going to find out what it is!*

3

Dumpster Queen

One of the good things about being home-schooled was that all the homeschool families often got together. This "support group" would meet at the church that Juliet and her family attended.

Sometimes these get-togethers were as dull as dishwater, as Joe said. But usually there would be play activities for the boys and girls while the adults talked about school projects. Later there would always be refreshments.

Today the children were playing out in the church parking lot when Flash Gordon said, "I hear your mom brought one of her famous chocolate cakes, Juliet."

Flash was ten years old, and his real name was Melvin. He got his nickname because he could go so fast in his wheelchair. Now Flash cut a wheelie in his chair. He had developed very strong arms from pushing the chair around. Then he stopped in front of Juliet and said, "Your mom makes the best chocolate cakes."

"Like your mom makes the best blueberry pies." Juliet smiled at him. She liked Flash a lot. He never complained about being in a wheelchair. In fact, he was one of the most cheerful boys she had ever met. He would often say, "You just watch. One of these days God's going to make me well. Then I'm going to walk again."

Just then Billy Rollins shouted, "Hey, look over there! There she is! The witch!"

Juliet looked across the parking lot. Butcher Knife Annie was walking past, pulling her red wagon.

"Old Billy can't be happy unless he's putting somebody down," Flash said in a disgusted voice. "Why doesn't he leave that poor old woman alone?"

"Do you know her?"

"I just know about her—like you do."

"Well, I think it's awful the way some kids make fun of her," Juliet said. "I'd like to bop that Billy Rollins right in the snoot."

"Why don't you?" Flash grinned happily. "Come on. I'll back you up."

Flash's wheelchair seemed to skim over the ground. Juliet had to run to keep up.

A small group of boys and girls was already

gathered around the old woman and her wagon.

"Billy Rollins," Juliet said at once, "why don't you just leave her alone!"

"What business is it of yours, Too Smart Jones?"

Billy Rollins, Juliet thought, was not a pleasant boy. And she had long ago decided that the worst thing about Billy was that he was so selfish. He always wanted to be the center of attention.

Billy looked around now to see if everybody was watching him. "I'm not afraid of you, Butcher Knife Annie," he said.

The elderly woman was wearing her usual dress—a worn one that dragged on the sidewalk. It was muddy around the hem and not too clean anywhere else. She had on a gray sweater with two large holes in it and had pulled her floppy hat down firmly as far as her ears.

"Get away and leave me alone," Butcher Knife Annie said hoarsely.

"What you going to do, Annie? Cut me up with that butcher knife?" Billy Rollins jeered. He danced around her. "Go ahead," he said. "Pull out that butcher knife."

"Leave her alone, Billy," Flash said. "She's not bothering you."

Juliet took a step toward Butcher Knife Annie. She said, "I'm sorry he's being so mean."

Billy Rollins paid no attention to Juliet or to Flash. "Come on, Annie, show us what kind of garbage you got in that wagon of yours."

Billy began to pull things out of the wagon and throw them on the sidewalk.

"Leave my stuff alone!" Annie tried to pull the wagon away, but the children still stood in a circle all around her.

This only made Billy laugh. Some other children began laughing and teasing and making fun of the old woman, too.

Juliet was usually a very sweet, calm girl, but she did have a temper. And now it bubbled over. She pushed Billy Rollins away from the wagon. "Leave her stuff alone, or I'll bop you right between the eyes!"

Billy staggered backward and frowned. "Don't you push me, Too Smart Jones, or I'll give you what for!"

"All you like to do is hurt people or make fun of people!" Juliet cried. "Go away and leave her alone! Now!"

Billy winked at Jack Tanner, one of his best friends. "Well, Jack," he said, "it looks like Too Smart Jones is going to protect all the butcher knife carriers in town."

"Billy, how would you feel if you were her?" Juliet asked. She lowered her voice. "She's just a poor old woman. Now leave her *alone.*"

But Billy Rollins was not finished. "Hey, maybe Too Smart's going to join up with Annie. You going to get a little red wagon and pull it around town, Too Smart?"

Some of the children laughed, and that made Juliet more angry. "You hush!" she said.

"Maybe you can join Butcher Knife Annie in the nut house. That's where she's going. The nut house."

Juliet had been watching Annie as this was going on. She saw the old woman's face grow pale beneath its coating of dirt. *She's frightened,* Juliet thought. This made her angrier still. "You don't know what you're talking about, Billy Rollins!"

"Sure I do," Billy jeered. "My dad says he and some other people are going to clean up the streets in this town. Old woman," he said, "you're going to the nut house."

Suddenly Chili Williams was beside Butcher Knife Annie's red wagon. Flash Gordon in his wheelchair closed in from the other side.

"That's enough!" Chili said. "Ma'am, you just go on along. Don't you pay no attention to these guys."

"Well, I don't know about that," Billy said. "Maybe I'm just not through with Butcher Knife Annie yet."

And then Chili Williams grabbed Billy by the arm. He twisted it. "You're through all right," Chili said with a grin. "Unless you want me to break this here arm, you better shush up!"

"Don't break his arm, Chili," Flash said. "Just hang onto him until we get her started with the wagon."

Juliet was more upset than she could remember ever being before. She hurried to say, "I'm sorry about all this, Annie—"

But Annie was shuffling off down the sidewalk, pulling the red wagon. She did not even answer.

Slowly Juliet walked over to the back step of the church. She sat down and began to think. She was wondering about Butcher Knife Annie. She was wondering what it would be like to be old. And to live in a shack. And to have no friends. And to be made fun of by children.

Juliet looked far down the sidewalk to where the old woman scurried along, pulling the red wagon after her. *I wonder what she was like when she wasn't old. I wonder what she was like when she was a girl like me. Could I wind up like Butcher Knife Annie someday?*

Juliet paid no attention to the other youngsters. They were playing again. She tried to think of how Annie would look if she had a bath, and clean clothes, and her hair fixed. And that very moment, Too Smart Jones began to make plans.

That night after Juliet went to bed, she lay for a long time, still thinking about ways to help Butcher Knife Annie. She decided she needed God's help.

"Lord," she said, "the pastor said last week that You know what people are thinking. You know what everybody in the world is thinking right now. Well, Lord, I'm thinking about Butcher Knife Annie. I don't even know her real name, but You do. Please show me how to be a friend to her. Lord, don't let her get sent to the mental hospital."

She listened as an owl somewhere outside her window called softly, *"To-whit. To-whoo!"* Then she said, "Nobody else is going to help her. None of the rest of the kids, anyway. And it doesn't look like the grown-ups are going to help either—unless Mom and Dad do. Lord, I know You love her, and I do want You to help me be a friend to her. Is that all right, Lord?"

Juliet waited, and finally a feeling of peace came over her. "Well, I'm going to take that for a yes. So I'm asking You in the name of Jesus —do something for Butcher Knife Annie."

4

Juliet's Scare

Every weekday morning, Juliet and Joe got up early, cleaned their rooms, and went down to breakfast. Afterward, they went at once to their study room and began their schoolwork. When they had started being homeschooled, Joe had said, "It'll be neat having Mom for a teacher. We'll have an easy time."

That had not been exactly the way it was, however. Mrs. Jones was the kindest of women, but she was strict in the classroom. She worked hard planning their lessons and their projects. And she made sure that they worked hard, too. Her tests were harder than any they had ever had in public school.

But the support group's field trips were always fun. Juliet and her brother managed to go on as many of them as possible. Often their mother was one of the parents who went along. Mr. Jones joined in whenever he could spare time from his job. The homeschooled children had been to every museum around Oakwood. They had seen Civil War reenactments. They had visited factories and businesses of every sort. Their heads were crammed full of information about their town and their county.

One Thursday morning, Juliet finished her latest project. She had been collecting pictures of American heroes. The walls were covered with them. The pictures went all the way back to George Washington. Her last picture was one of John Glenn, who had made his second flight into space at the age of seventy-seven.

Joe had wanted her to collect pictures of sports people, but Juliet had said no. "No, they're not heroes. They may be good people, but my heroes have to give something to their country. Or do something real good for somebody else. Like him." She'd pointed to the picture of a man that Joe said he did not recognize. "That's Dr. Flemming. He discovered penicillin. Now, he's a hero. Think of how many lives he saved."

With a sigh, Juliet leaned back and looked at the walls. "That looks good. And it's about all the heroes I've got room for."

"Unless you start using the dining room walls."

Joe's own project was different. He'd been

using a tape recorder to interview all of the older people in the neighborhood. He held up one of his tapes and said, "Look here. I got this tape from old Mr. Dugan. Boy, does he know a lot of stuff! He remembers back when there wasn't even a paved road in this county. Nothing but dirt roads. I'm glad we got past that."

"That's a good project you've got going there, Joe. Maybe we could type it up and put it into a booklet. Then other people can read it."

"I'll let you do that. I just like to talk to 'em and find out about what went on a long time ago."

The two worked on their studies until noon. After lunch they did their chores. As soon as Juliet was finished, she said, "Mom, I'm going out for a while. OK?"

"Where you going this time, Juliet?"

"Oh, I don't know. Maybe down to the park."

"All right, but you be home by four thirty."
"I will."

Juliet shivered a little as she walked down the street. The air was getting colder, she thought. She zipped up her coat and pulled her toboggan cap down firmly over her ears. "Bet it's going to snow," she said, looking up into the sky. "I hope we have a white Christmas this year."

She started for the park, but before she got there she changed her mind. She'd been thinking a lot about Butcher Knife Annie, and now suddenly she had an idea. *I think I'll just go see if I can catch a glimpse of her anywhere. Maybe I'll even get a chance to talk to her.*

Juliet had heard that Annie roamed the alleys behind the food stores every afternoon. So she went straight to the downtown area and started walking through the alleys by the supermarkets. She did not see the old woman anywhere. But as she went past the alley that ran between a large office building and Smith's Hardware Store, Juliet stopped.

There she was. Butcher Knife Annie was walking through that alley, pulling her faded red wagon. Her back was toward Juliet, and her head was down. She was moving slowly, as if she was very tired.

Juliet thought, *I bet she's worn out from pulling that wagon all the way into town and back every day.* She hesitated for a moment, not knowing what to do. Then she said, "Well, the Bible says he that would have a friend must show himself friendly. And I guess that means *her*self, too. So here I go."

With a determined step, Juliet Jones marched down the alley toward the old woman.

Now Butcher Knife Annie dropped the handle of the wagon and bent over to prowl in a large cardboard box behind the hardware store. She was pulling out some object when Juliet said, "Hello, Annie. How are you today?"

The old woman whirled around. She had the knife out before Juliet could even blink. "Why are you sneaking up on me?" she asked angrily.

"I wasn't—"

Annie took a step forward and waved the butcher knife. She took another step, holding it up in a threatening way. Her eyes looked wild. She was muttering something under her breath.

All Juliet could see was the big, sharp looking knife. Fear came over her, and she gave a small cry. She turned and raced out of the alley. She did not stop running until she had gotten all the way to the edge of town. There she stopped and leaned against a big oak tree. Her breath was coming in sobs, and her heart was beating like a machine gun.

"What in the world is the matter with you?"

Juliet looked up to see Jenny White and Delores Del Rio coming toward her. Delores and her brother, Samuel, lived in a house on the outskirts of town.

Delores was a very good friend. She was nine years old, the same age as Jenny. Right now her large brown eyes were filled with concern. "You look sick, Juliet. Are you? What's wrong?"

Jenny looked closely at Juliet's face and said, "Why, you're white as a sheet!"

"I'm all right," Juliet said, still trying to catch her breath. "I'm all right."

"You don't look all right to me," Delores said. "You'd better come to our house if you don't feel good."

"I'm all right. I feel all right," Juliet repeated. She did not want to tell the girls what had happened. She took a deep breath and tried to laugh. "I guess I just ran a little bit too hard. It took my breath."

"What were you running so fast for?" Jenny asked curiously.

"Yeah, you going out for track or something?" Delores asked.

"Oh, I like to jog now and then. Dad does that, you know. We all have to keep in shape to please him."

Jenny looked at Delores, and Delores looked at Jenny. Juliet was sure they were both thinking, *This isn't like Juliet.*

But Delores said, "We're going to my house and play dress up, Juliet. Why don't you come with us?"

Quickly Juliet nodded. "Sure. I'd like that."

The three girls headed east until they got to a large two-story house surrounded by a black iron fence—the Del Rio home. When they went inside, they found Mr. Del Rio and his wife sitting in the kitchen. They were the grandparents of Samuel and Delores. The children had lost their parents in an automobile accident.

"Ah, it is good to see you," Mr. Del Rio said. He was a fine looking man with snow-white hair and merry dark eyes. "Sit down here. My wife is a terrible cook, but she will give you something that you may be able to eat."

Mrs. Del Rio gave her husband a scornful glance. "Ha! You seem to get enough of it down, Ramon!"

"That is true. I was only teasing. Today she is baking some sopaipillas."

"Oh, good! I love sopaipillas!" Jenny cried.

Juliet was somewhat over her scare by now. "I could eat some, too," she said. "I tried to make some the other day, but they didn't turn out very good. Maybe you could give me your recipe."

Mrs. Del Rio laughed. "I write nothing down. I will just show you how. That's the best way to learn. I make some more right now."

While the girls were gathered around the stove watching Mrs. Del Rio make sopaipillas, Mr. Del Rio sat reading the *Oakwood Gazette*. Suddenly he said, "There's a letter to the editor in the newspaper from Mr. Harold Rollins."

"Oh, him!" Jenny said. "What does he say now?"

Harold Rollins was Billy Rollins father. He was almost as unpleasant and hard to get along with as Billy was himself.

"His letter says: 'Something must be done about the people that are roaming the streets

41

of Oakwood. The town is filling up with people who have no jobs. I think we all know that such people as this can be dangerous. I propose that the city clear our streets of these persons at once."

Mr. Del Rio put down his paper. His eyes were puzzled. "Who does he mean? I haven't seen any of these people. Who are these people he talks about?"

"I think he just means Butcher Knife Annie," Jenny said. "Billy said his father is going to get her sent away to a mental hospital."

"Who is this Butcher Knife Annie?" Mrs. Del Rio asked as she put down a panful of hot sopaipillas. "Who is this with such a strange name?"

Juliet said, "It's not really her name. She's an old lady who lives by herself over by the river."

"Oh, is she the one who pulls the wagon?" Mr. Del Rio nodded. "Then I've seen her. A strange woman. But she seems harmless enough."

Juliet thought about the knife. "But Mr. Rollins . . ."

"Well, I would not be in favor of Mr. Rollins's proposal," Mr. Del Rio said firmly. "As long as she is just a harmless old woman . . ."

"Why don't you write a letter to the newspaper and say so, Mr. Del Rio?"

"I believe I will. Perhaps this Mr. Rollins is making a big mistake."

The girls filled themselves with sopaipillas, and then they went upstairs.

The attic of the Del Rio house was a delight. It was large and had windows at both ends. It was filled with trunks of old-fashioned clothes—some must have been one hundred years old. The girls liked nothing better than to put on the long dresses. They had to pin them up, of course, but that was not a problem. There were large bonnets too and hats and shawls and coats. And there were shoes! Most of the shoes had high heels, and the three girls loved that.

After they had played for a long time, Juliet heard a voice from below. "Delores, you have company."

The girls hurriedly put away the clothes and rushed down the stairs. They found Samuel and Joe in the kitchen, wolfing down sopaipillas.

Joe spoke with his mouth full. "We're going out to the park to play soccer. The three of you want to come along?"

Juliet answered for them all. "That would be fun."

"Then put on your warm clothes, Delores," Mrs. Del Rio said. "It's getting very cold outside."

"All right, Grandmother. I will." Delores ran off to get what she needed.

As the youngsters headed out the front door, Joe asked, "Where you been all afternoon, Juliet? I've been looking for you."

"I think she got sick," Delores said.

"Sick!" Joe looked at her. "Are you sick, Juliet?"

"No. I just ran a little bit too fast."

It was the truth—she *had* run a little too fast. But Juliet felt guilty. She knew that it was only a half-truth, and usually Juliet was an honest girl.

I'll tell Joe all about it when we get home, she thought. *But not now.*

5

Ducks

The soccer game in the park turned out to be great fun, as always. There were organized soccer teams in Oakwood, and some of the homeschool children took part in them. But Juliet liked it much better when a bunch of kids simply got together and kicked the ball around.

On one team were Joe and Juliet, Jenny White, and the Boyd twins, Helen and Ray. On the other side were Billy Rollins, Flash Gordon, Chili Williams, and Samuel and Delores.

For a while, they tried to keep score. But that didn't work for long because of all the arguments.

Helen and Ray were both spoiled. They were used to having their own way. When

Chili Williams kicked the ball out from between Ray's feet, Ray started protesting.

"That's a foul!"

But Chili laughed at him. "It's not a foul at all, Ray. You just got to learn to watch what you're doing."

Part of the fun of the game was watching Flash Gordon. He could not kick the ball, of course, but it was amazing what he *could* do! He kept wheeling his chair up and down the field. When he got close to the ball, he would simply lean over and smack it with his fist. It was kind of a mix of soccer and volleyball.

Juliet was the goalkeeper for their team. But when Samuel Del Rio kicked the ball straight at her, she covered her face and fell on the ground.

"Juliet," Ray yelled, "you're supposed to block the ball, not fall down and cry."

"You're a fine goalie!" Helen Boyd said. "I want to be the goalkeeper."

Juliet was happy about that. "That's fine with me, Helen. You go right ahead."

On the very next play, Flash Gordon reached over and smacked the ball with his fist. It hit Helen right in the stomach.

"*Oof!*" Helen said. She dropped to the ground, holding her stomach. Then she began to cry.

"You did that on purpose, Flash!" Ray said.

"I sure did. I hit the ball right toward the

goal. That's what you're supposed to do in soccer. I wasn't trying to hit *her*." Then Flash grinned. "Come on. Let's play ball. She's all right."

"You might have crippled her," Ray said.

Jenny said, "Let me be the goalie."

So the game went on. Some goals were scored, but many times the ball just went flying high in the air toward nothing.

"You trying to kick a goal over the moon?" Chili laughed one time when Joe sent the ball fifty feet in the air.

"That wouldn't be a bad idea," Joe said.

When they were all tired, Helen said, "I'm going down to Beenie's Hot Dog Shop for some hot chocolate. Anybody want to go with me?"

Some had money, and some did not, but Flash said, "Everyone give me your money, and I'll see that everybody gets some hot chocolate."

Everyone trusted Flash, so off they went toward Beenie's. Flash did see to it that they all had hot chocolate. They also had a hot dog apiece.

There was a great deal of smearing mustard, ketchup, and chowchow on the hot dogs. Beenie himself finally grumbled, "I don't make no profit off of you guys. You eat up enough mustard and chowchow to take all the profit out of it."

After they had eaten their hot dogs and

downed the hot chocolate, they started back to the soccer field. This time they took a shortcut through the park.

Suddenly Helen Boyd said, "There's that awful old woman. Over by the pond."

Quickly Juliet looked toward the pond. There sat Butcher Knife Annie on a bench. She had a sack between her feet, and a great flock of ducks was gathered around her.

"My daddy's going to get rid of her," Billy Rollins said loudly. "Did you see the letter in the paper that he wrote?"

"I saw it," Samuel said. "And my grandfather's going to answer it. Your dad can't run people out of town just because he doesn't like them."

"That's right," Chili Williams said. "We were real poor when we first came here. Nobody tried to run *us* out of town."

"That's different," Billy said. "Your people had a house."

"Annie's got a house, too," Juliet put in.

"A house! You call that place where she lives a house?" Billy said scornfully. "It's just a shack. It doesn't even have a bathroom."

Juliet watched Butcher Knife Annie while the others had more things to say. She saw, too, that some of the ducks were mallards with bright green feathers. Some of them, she knew, were Muscovy ducks. They were heavy and rather ugly with wattles on their bills and their heads. But her father had told her that they laid wonderful eggs. "We used to have Muscovys when I was a boy," he'd said. "It was my job to go out and find the eggs, and were they ever good."

Juliet saw Annie reach into the large paper sack between her feet. She held out pieces of something to the ducks. Maybe bread? Then the ducks pushed close and took them right out of her hand. A great deal of quacking was going on as the ducks all jostled to get close to her.

One duck even jumped up onto the bench beside the old woman. Even from where she stood, Juliet could see, for the first time, a smile on Butcher Knife Annie's face. She didn't seem to know that anyone was watching her.

Juliet thought, *She doesn't look like the same woman that I saw back in the alley. I wonder which is the real Annie—the one that loves ducks or the one that threatens people with a butcher knife.*

Billy Rollins said, "I guess ducks are the only things that could be her friend—she smells so bad."

The Boyd twins thought that was very funny. They laughed loudly.

But Juliet didn't think it was funny. "You ought not to talk that way about an old woman," she said.

"You still sticking up for her?" Billy Rollins

said. "Too Smart Jones, the dumpster queen. That's what we'll call you."

The Boyd twins, too, started to make fun of Juliet for defending Butcher Knife Annie.

But Jenny White looked worried. "I'm afraid of her. I'd hate to meet her in a dark alley at night."

"What would you be doing in a dark alley at night?" Juliet asked, trying to be funny. To be afraid of Annie seemed rather foolish to her. But then she remembered how terrified she herself had been at the sight of that knife. She never wanted to see it again! She was glad when the group walked on and began playing soccer again.

After the game broke up, Joe went off with Samuel, saying, "I'll see you back at the house."

"You want to come home with me, Juliet?" Flash said. "Mom baked a blueberry pie today."

"I'd better not. I've got to go home pretty soon. But thanks a lot, Flash. Save me a piece of pie."

Juliet waited until the others had gone their different ways. Then she turned back to the park.

Keeping herself hidden behind some bushes, she looked out and saw that Annie was still sitting on the bench. The old woman was as still as a statue. She seemed to be looking out over the water. Some of the ducks were still there, but there seemed to be no more food. Most of them had gone back to swimming out on the pond.

As Juliet looked on, Annie got up slowly. She moved as if her back hurt, and she could not seem to straighten up. She picked up the handle of her wagon then and plodded out of the park.

Watching her go, Juliet began having an argument with herself. She did not feel at all good about the way she had misled her mother. She also knew she had not been completely honest with Jenny and Delores.

Finally she sat down on the bench where Annie had been sitting. She looked at the ducks. They saw her and came quacking back. "I don't have anything for you ducks," she told them. "I'll bring you something tomorrow— maybe."

The sun was starting downward in the sky, and still Juliet sat there. She was a girl who dearly loved mysteries. Now she thought, as she had many times before, *Who is Butcher Knife Annie? What is she doing here?* Questions ran through her mind.

Finally she said, "My mind's made up. I'm going to learn more about her. Maybe tomorrow I'll follow her, but this time I won't let her see me. It's going to take a long time to get to the bottom of this. But I'll find out about Butcher Knife Annie, or my name isn't Too Smart Jones!"

6

Juliet
Gets Caught

Saturday morning Juliet woke up feeling great. Saturday was the one day she could do anything she wanted. No lessons today and very few chores.

She lay in bed for a while simply enjoying the thought of having a day to do exactly what she pleased. Her eyes ran around the room and over the stuffed animals that lined the walls. Her father had built shelves all around, just under the ceiling. One of the stuffed animals was Tigger, right out of *Winnie the Pooh*. He was practically worn out—she had carried him with her almost constantly while she was still just a toddler. He had gone through the washer many times. Tigger grinned down at her, his fur practically worn off by the many adventures that Juliet had put him through.

"Old Tigger," she murmured. "I remember

when I wouldn't go to sleep unless I had you in my hands. We had some good times together, didn't we, Tigger?"

Her eyes moved on to the next stuffed toy. It was a large teddy bear with close-set eyes. The bear seemed to be staring at her. It also was well worn.

"And there you are, Manny," she said. "You and I slept together a long time. I wonder if you ever get lonesome for me?" It had only been two years since Manny had been retired to the shelf, but Juliet still liked him.

Her latest stuffed friend was beside her pillow. He was a frog dressed in a tuxedo and a top hat. He had a silly looking grin on his face. He had been a present from her mother, who knew that even though she was growing up, Juliet still liked stuffed toys. His name was Ribbet.

Juliet perched Ribbet on her stomach. Holding him firmly in place, she said, "Ribbet, what are you good for?" She waited for him to answer. When he did not, she answered for him. It was a little game she played with all of her stuffed toys, giving them voices and carrying on conversations.

"I'm good for making you happy."

"Making me happy! Why, you're nothing but a stuffed toy!"

"But you love me, don't you? Give me some sugar!"

Juliet laughed and kissed Ribbet's ugly face. Then she rolled out of bed. "You can sleep for the rest of the day, but I'm not going to waste my whole Saturday."

After dressing, Juliet quickly cleaned up her room and went downstairs. She found that breakfast was already over. Her mother said, "I wanted to let you sleep late. You were up so late last night. What can I fix for your breakfast?"

"Pancakes."

"I thought so. I saved you some, so sit down, and I'll heat them up for you."

Nobody made pancakes as good as her mom, Juliet thought. When a stack sat before her, she dipped a knife into the yellow butter and spread it liberally.

Juliet ate three pancakes and two slices of Canadian bacon. Then she washed the dishes. After that she went to her room and just read for a while. She was reading "The Narnia Chronicles" by a man called C. S. Lewis. She could not wait to see how they turned out. They were fantasy, and Juliet loved fantasies.

Finally, with a sigh, she put a marker in her book, closed it, and put on her coat and cap. Then she picked up a tablet and a ballpoint pen and left the house, calling, "I'm going out to play for a while, Mom. Maybe I'll go over to Delores's—or maybe Jenny's."

"All right. Just be back for lunch."

Juliet walked quickly down the street, greeting the neighbors as she went. She knew that Joe was out in the woods with Samuel Del Rio and Chili Williams. They had told her she could go with them, but she had said no.

She reached town shortly and went into the variety store. She had saved up money to buy some jewelry. Now she went around looking at all the items. She saw only one piece that she liked. It was a ring with a red stone in it, and it cost only a dollar. She paid for the ring and put it on. When she got outside, she held her hand up, and the sun shone on the red stone. From time to time as she walked around looking into the store windows, she held up the ring and admired it.

And then, just as Juliet was about ready to turn and go back home, she saw Butcher Knife Annie. She watched as the old woman pulled her wagon down Oak Street. It seemed to be more heavily loaded than usual. From time to time she would turn into an alley.

Juliet began to follow Butcher Knife Annie, but she kept out of sight. She was determined to keep an eye on her. Just exactly how she would speak to her, she hadn't figured out yet. But she prayed again for the woman, and she was sure that God was going to show her how. *After all*, she thought as she kept well behind Annie, *I just want to be her friend.*

For a long time Juliet stayed behind Annie. The woman stopped at every dumpster, at every garbage can, at every pile of boxes. She went through them all, one at a time.

Once, when Juliet got a little closer, she saw something in the red wagon that surprised her. It was a gray cat, just quietly sitting and looking around. She thought, *I wonder if she just found that cat, or if it's hers.*

Juliet was more determined than ever to find out more about Butcher Knife Annie. She must have trailed her for nearly an hour. Her mind was completely set on what she was doing.

Suddenly hands grabbed her from behind. She screamed. She cried out, "Let me go!" Then she twisted around to see Billy Rollins and Ray Boyd.

"What do you mean sneaking up on me like that?"

Ray Boyd grinned broadly. "Looks like you're the one doing the sneaking."

"We've been watching you," Billy said. "You been following old Butcher Knife Annie there. What are you up to, Too Smart?"

"It's none of your business!"

"I know what she's doing," Ray said. "She's playing detective again. She always does that. You think Butcher Knife Annie's some kind of a criminal? Maybe there's a reward out for her."

Billy Rollins laughed. "Yeah, that would be cool. We could turn her in and split the reward three ways."

"She's not a criminal!"

"How do you know she's not?" Billy demanded. "You know something about her that we don't know?"

Juliet really knew little more than any of the other boys and girls. But she was still sure that the old woman was harmless.

Then Ray Boyd said, "Hey, Too Smart, you even kind of look like Annie." He reached over and pulled Juliet's toboggan cap down over her eyes. "If you don't take a bath, pretty soon you'll smell as bad as she does."

"Yeah, then you can be an alley woman, too. A garbage woman. Yeah, a garbage woman! The dumpster queen!"

Juliet felt herself growing very angry. She was still upset that the boys had caught her following Annie—and then had sneaked up on her as they had. She said, "Just go away and mind your own business!"

"I think we'd better go by and tell your mom," Ray Boyd said. His eyes were sparkling. "She'll probably want to know you're out in the alleys chasing around after an old lady with a butcher knife."

"You stay away from my house!"

"You're right, Ray. We'd better go tell her. Right away," Billy said.

Juliet knew he could tell that she was mad. And nothing pleased Billy more than to upset Too Smart Jones.

Juliet turned away. She paid no attention to their calls after her. *If they do tell Mom,* she said to herself unhappily, *she'll make me stop investigating this case.* She didn't want that to happen.

She saw that Butcher Knife Annie had disappeared. Which way had she gone?

For a while Juliet looked around for her. But soon she thought, *I've got some time yet. I think I'll go find Annie's house. I won't go in or anything like that. I'll just sneak up on it. And who knows what I'll find out?*

Juliet still was upset by what Billy and Ray had said they were going to do. But she tried to put it out of her mind. "They won't tell," she decided. "They won't tell. They were just being mean."

She quickly took off toward the poor part of town. Even as she did, she felt something cold touch her face. It surprised her, and she looked up. Snowflakes were drifting down. "Snow," she said. "I love snow. Maybe there'll be enough to make a snowman."

But right away Juliet's mind went to other things beside snowmen. She was going to find out about Butcher Knife Annie. She made her way steadily toward Shanty Town, down streets that were turning white with snow.

7

More Detective Work

Oakwood was like many other towns. The people who had a lot of money lived in one part of town. The people with not so much money lived in another. And far away, across the railroad tracks and down by the river, the very poor people lived.

As Juliet crossed the tracks, she thought, *I've never been in this part of town.* She had heard things about Shanty Town, though. *It's a little bit scary here,* she decided.

For a few moments she stood on a little hill, looking down at the small houses between the tracks and the river. Smoke rose out of chimneys into the cold air. Then Juliet nodded her head firmly. "I'll just go take a look," she said under her breath. "How can that hurt anything?"

Juliet walked into Shanty Town, feeling a

little nervous. The main street made twists and turns like a snake. It was as if it had once been just a winding path.

She passed a small house covered with tar paper. A half dozen children were playing out in front. They all wore coats that did not seem to fit. And they all peered at her curiously without speaking as she passed by. She smiled, but only two of the smaller children smiled back.

One of them—a boy with a dirty face—waved at her.

Juliet waved and said, "Hi."

He did not return her greeting, though.

Juliet continued on. The crooked street made a sharp turn. And there in somebody's front yard stood a woman. She was cooking something in a huge black pot over a wood fire. She was stirring it with a stick, and at first Juliet thought it was something to eat. But as she got closer, she saw that it was *clothing* that the woman was boiling. Juliet had never seen anyone wash clothes like that. She thought, *I've never been thankful for our washer and dryer. I will be now. That's so easy, and this is so hard.*

"Hello," she said shyly.

The woman gave her a not very friendly look but finally nodded. "Hello," she mumbled. Her hands were blue with the cold.

As she spoke, a big dog came around the house, showing his teeth.

"Get back there, Roscoe!" the woman said. The dog started to pass her, still growling. She gave him a kick. "I said get back!"

The dog slunk away, his fangs stilled bared. He crept under the house, but he kept his eyes fixed on Juliet.

"Does he bite?" Juliet asked.

"He bites strangers."

That was enough for Juliet, for she was certainly a stranger. She started on down the street, walking faster. On an empty lot, some small children were playing a game with sticks and a ball. She watched them for a while and wondered what it must be like to live in Shanty Town. She wondered what it would be like to have only sticks to play with. She thought, *I hope I never find out. It must be awful!*

She hurried on. For a while she just wandered here and there. Chili had told her what Butcher Knife Annie's shack looked like. But she saw several that looked like that. She could not be sure.

"Hello, Juliet."

The sound of a voice calling her name stopped Juliet in her tracks. She turned around, and her eyes flew open with surprise. "Why, hello, Mary," she said. "I didn't know you lived around here."

Mary Sullivan was on a softball team that Juliet and her support group had played against several times. She was a quiet girl, however, and Juliet had never done more than just say hi.

"Do you live around here, Mary?"

"Right over there—in that house. The green one." Mary pointed.

The house was, indeed, painted an ugly shade of apple green. It seemed as though every house in Shanty Town had several little children playing out in front. Mary's house did, too.

"What are you doing down here?" Mary Sullivan asked. She was wearing a purple skirt and a man's gray sweater that swallowed her. The long sleeves were pushed up, and her hands were bluish from the cold.

Juliet suddenly felt wrong having warm mittens when Mary had none. She felt like taking them off and giving them to the girl. But that did not seem the right thing to do, either.

And she didn't know how to answer Mary's question. She couldn't say, "I'm looking for Butcher Knife Annie." Then Mary would want to know why. Juliet was sure her face was turning red. She finally said, "Well, I was out for a walk and . . ."

"Not many people come for walks down here," Mary said.

Again Juliet did not know what to say. She had known that Mary Sullivan came from a poor family. Her clothes were enough to show that. But she hadn't known Mary lived here— in Shanty Town! She tried hard to think of something to say, but nothing came to mind. "Well, I guess I'd better get going, Mary. I'll see you later."

Quickly Juliet left, glad to be free from that conversation. One thing that did come to her mind was the clothes she had on. They were so expensive when compared to the clothes that Mary Sullivan wore. Mary's dress looked like a hand-me-down, perhaps from an older sister. Juliet had never really thought much about what it was like to be very poor. But she was thinking about it now.

Ten minutes later, she was about ready to give up when she walked up a little hill and looked down toward the river again. There, in the middle of a small clump of trees, sat a tiny shack. "That's it!" Juliet whispered. "It's just exactly like Chili said it was."

She went down the hill cautiously, ready to turn and run in case Annie and her knife appeared. But she saw no one. Maybe nobody was at home. The door to the shack faced the river, so she went around to the side, keeping herself hidden as much as possible by a growth of hackberry trees.

Carefully, almost holding her breath, Juliet walked up to the house. The shack had never been painted. It was made of bare boards that were weathered into a pale silver color. The roof was patched with some different-colored shingles. There were two windows on the side. The glass of one was broken out, and that window was covered with cardboard.

Juliet crept closer.

Carefully she lifted her head by the good window. She saw, first, that there were no curtains. She picked up an old bucket, turned it upside down, and climbed up on it. The bucket teetered, and she held onto the outside of the window. The glass was dirty, and she could not see much. She did see, however, that no one was home.

Stepping down off the bucket, Juliet went around to the door. It was standing partly open. *No one would go off and leave a house open in cold weather like this,* she thought. *The wind must have blown it open.*

At that moment the wind caught the door again and blew it open all the way.

Juliet stepped up close and peered inside. There wasn't much furniture. A cot with a faded striped mattress stood in one corner. A wooden box that may have been used as a table was in the middle. And there was only one chair. It was an old one with a leg that had been repaired.

A single light bulb hung down on a wire. The shack had a small sink. Some boxes were nailed on the wall to form a cupboard. And there was a woodstove. Juliet reached out to pull the door shut and keep out the cold.

Just as she did, however, she noticed another box to the right of the door. Maybe it too was used as a table. She saw what looked like a photograph album lying right on top of the box.

Juliet felt the urge to look at it. She would not even have to go into the house to get the album, Too Smart Jones told herself. It was within her reach.

Maybe that picture album would tell me what I need to know about Annie, she thought. The wind whistled around the chimney as she stood there uncertainly.

Finally she reached in for the album. She felt guilty about what she was doing. This was a lot like snooping. As a matter of fact, it *was* snooping. But she had gone this far, so she would go ahead. She stood at the door and quickly turned the pages.

Most of the pictures were of a nice looking couple, not very old. The snapshots seemed to have been taken in faraway places, not around Oakwood. When she came to the last page, she found a picture of the man and the woman that was the same as one she had seen earlier in the album.

Once again Juliet was thinking hard. *If I take this extra picture, maybe I can use it to find out who Annie is. And I might be able to help her,* she told herself.

Still, Juliet felt it was not quite right to take the picture. For some reason she remembered her Sunday school teacher saying, "We can always find some reason for doing what we want to do—no matter how wrong it is . . ."

But Too Smart Jones said aloud, "I need to do this. I want to be Annie's friend. And I've got to find out about her before I can be a friend. I'll bring back the picture as soon as I find out."

With a guilty feeling, Juliet slipped the picture into her pocket. She put the album back on the box, shut the door, and walked away quickly. Her heart was beating a little faster than it usually did. She hurried back through Shanty Town and kept watching for Annie. But she did not see her.

As soon as Juliet was back on the "good side" of the tracks, her heart grew lighter—until she began to think about what she had done. *I know Mom and Dad wouldn't like it. It was a lot like going into her house and stealing something,* she thought. *But I'm really going to take the picture back as soon as I find out something about it. I really am.*

Somehow this thought did not comfort Juliet much. One time, she almost turned around and ran back to return the picture. But she didn't.

As she walked on toward home, she took out the picture and studied it. *I wonder if this is a picture of Annie a long time ago. And I wonder who the man is.*

She had no idea how this picture would help her, but it was a start.

8

Trouble for Juliet

Juliet always enjoyed her Sunday school class. Her teacher, Mrs. Gibson, was the PE teacher at the middle school. She was a pretty lady with coppery red hair and blue green eyes that Juliet had always admired. She was very interested in each member of the class. She sometimes invited them to her house. Best of all, she was a fine teacher and knew the Bible very well. Usually she kept the attention of the class.

This Sunday morning, however, Mrs. Gibson was having trouble. Billy Rollins and Ray Boyd always had to be warned several times to be quiet. But today they were worse than usual. They whispered and laughed until finally Mrs. Gibson had to say rather sternly, "Billy and Ray, I'm going to ask you one more time to be quiet. You're disturbing the class."

"Who? Us?" Billy grinned. "I don't think we were disturbing the class. Do you, Ray?"

Ray, who always followed whatever Billy started, tried to look innocent. "Why, no, Mrs. Gibson. We were just talking about the lesson."

Everyone knew that was not true. Mrs. Gibson knew it. She frowned at them. "I still say you'll have to be quiet while the lesson is going on."

Billy Rollins rolled his eyes. Then he looked over toward Juliet, and he grinned. "Mrs. Gibson, you're real interested in all of us kids, aren't you?"

"Of course I am, Billy."

"Well, you ought to pay special attention to one member of your class who hasn't been behaving right."

Mrs. Gibson looked hard at Billy. "We're not going to talk about people in this class, Billy."

"Oh, I'm not going to do that. It's just that I'm worried about one of the members."

"Then you ought to go to that person alone. That's what the Bible says. If you have a problem with someone, go to him alone and tell him what it is."

"Oh, I've tried to do that, but it didn't do any good, Mrs. Gibson. She won't listen." Now Billy looked straight at Juliet. "Will you, Juliet?"

"I don't know what you're talking about, Billy!" Juliet said sharply.

"I'm talking about how you go sneaking down into Shanty Town."

Jenny White gave a small gasp. She was sitting right next to Juliet, and she turned to stare at her friend. "Did you do that, Juliet?"

Juliet was furious. "You're nothing but a tattletale, Billy Rollins!"

"I'm just trying to help," Billy said innocently.

Mrs. Gibson tried to put a stop to the arguing. "Boys and girls—"

"Yeah," Ray Boyd said. "That's dangerous down there. Those Shanty Town people do all kinds of bad things."

Jenny looked very upset. She seemed to forget that she was in Sunday school, and she said, almost harshly, "Juliet, you *promised* me you wouldn't try to find out anything else about Butcher Knife Annie!"

A puzzled look was on Mrs. Gibson's face now. "And w*ho* is Butcher Knife Annie?"

"She's a crazy old woman who goes around carrying a butcher knife," Billy said. "She says she'll kill people with it. That's what she really says."

"And some people in town are going to have her put into a mental hospital. Maybe even in jail." Ray Boyd grinned at Juliet and added, "Juliet likes her, though. She wants to be just like her."

"You hush up, Ray Boyd!"

Obviously pleased that they were getting Juliet angry, Billy Rollins went on. "Yep, she's going to be the dumpster queen, Juliet is."

The argument had gotten out of hand, but Mrs. Gibson finally put an end to it by saying firmly, "That's *enough*, students. There'll be no more talk about this. And, Billy, I mean you especially!"

Billy Rollins let an offended look cross his face. "I was just trying to help, Mrs. Gibson. I mean, when one of your friends is in trouble, you try to help. Well, I was just worried about Juliet going down to the dangerous part of town."

"I said that's enough about this! Now let's get back to the lesson. Paul was in prison, and yet he was trusting God . . ."

After Sunday school, Jenny and Juliet walked out of the classroom together.

Billy was right behind them. He said, "That was a good Sunday school class, wasn't it, Juliet? Bet you learned a lot."

The girls paid no attention to him.

"He's so mean," Juliet said. "Why does he have to be like that?"

"I know he's mean sometimes, but he's right this time," Jenny said. A worried look was still on her face. "You *promised* me you wouldn't go following after Butcher Knife Annie."

"I didn't exactly promise."

"You did too!"

"Well, I had my fingers crossed behind my back."

"Juliet, that doesn't mean *any*thing! You know better than that!"

Actually, Juliet did know better than that, and she was suddenly ashamed. "I know. That was really lying, and it was wrong. I'm sorry, and I'm never going to do that again."

"I'm glad to hear that," Jenny said. "But you *were* in Shanty Town looking for Butcher Knife Annie, weren't you?"

"Yes. I was. There's something *strange* about her, Jenny. I want to find out what it is."

"There's nothing you can do about her, Juliet. There are all kinds of people in trouble in the world. And not all of them live down by the river in Shanty Town, either."

Jenny and Juliet went to sit with their families for the church service. Juliet took the hymnbook and began to sing the songs. She could not sing as well as Jenny—or even as well as Joe, which irritated her—but she always did the best she could.

The service went on. Juliet was still upset over what had taken place in the Sunday school class. She was not thinking much about worshiping God, so she was somewhat surprised to look up and see that the pastor was ready to begin his sermon.

Brother Prince was a nice looking man with light hair and blue eyes. He was short but strongly built. And he was a fine preacher. He looked out over his congregation and smiled.

"I'm glad you're all here this morning. My sermon will be about how Jesus wants us to treat others. Some sermons, we may feel, are for someone else, but every one of us has to live with other people," he said. "I'll begin by reading to you one of the best-known stories in the whole Bible, the story of the Good Samaritan."

Juliet knew that story. But she opened her Bible and followed along as the minister read the story again.

When he had finished reading and had prayed a brief prayer, he began to preach.

Juliet listened to him talk about the Bible verses. Someone had asked Jesus, "Who is my neighbor?" And Jesus told a story about a Jewish man who had been beaten by thieves and left for dead along the roadside.

Mr. Prince said, "Some so-called good people came by and saw this poor man, but they walked right past. One of them even crossed to the other side of the road to get away from him. He felt no need to offer help.

"But then a Samaritan came along. Remember, in those days no Jew would have anything to do with a Samaritan. And yet it was a Samaritan who stopped and helped the Jewish man who had been beaten. He bandaged his wounds. He took him to an inn. And he arranged to pay for his care."

Juliet was still listening carefully as Brother Prince came to the end of his message. "Who is *our* neighbor? Our neighbor is anyone we see who is in trouble. It doesn't matter what the color of his skin is. It doesn't matter whether he has more or less than we have. Nothing matters except that he has a need and Jesus wants to help him.

"Sometimes," he said, "Jesus uses people to do the helping. As a matter of fact, I think He usually does. So I'm going to ask you a question. Have *you* met anyone who needs help? Second question: Are you doing everything you can to help them?"

Juliet always liked Brother Prince's sermons, but this one seemed to be pointed especially at her.

As the last hymn was sung, she was singing the words, but she was thinking, *I'm going to ask Mom and Dad to help me with Annie. I'll talk to them at dinner today.* This made her feel better at once. She had not felt at all good about keeping something secret from her parents. She repeated her plan to herself as she walked down the church steps. *Mom and Dad will know what to do,* she thought, and suddenly she felt very cheerful.

Dinner at the Jones house on Sundays was always a masterpiece. Mrs. Jones had learned how to do most of the cooking before they went to church. Then, when they got home, all she had to do was to take the things out of the oven.

Juliet finished setting the table, and the Jones family sat down.

As soon as Mr. Jones had asked the blessing, Joe reached for the fried chicken and grabbed two legs from the top of the pile.

"You can't have both of those!" Juliet cried. "I like the leg, too, you know!"

Joe grinned at her. "Why don't you eat the wings?" He was holding a fat chicken leg in each hand and waving them around. "You wouldn't want to deprive me of the part I like best."

"Joe, stop teasing Juliet and give her one of those chicken legs," their father ordered. He looked very handsome today in his new blue shirt with a maroon tie to match.

Everybody knew that Joe loved fried chicken legs, but he had no hope of getting both. Scowling, he handed one of them over to Juliet.

And then he muttered, "If you knew what Juliet's been doing, you wouldn't let her have *any* chicken, much less the best part."

Juliet's heart sank. She knew what Joe was going to say. She tried to speak up before he could tell, but Joe jumped into relating what had happened in Sunday school class.

Juliet's father looked at her with a frown. "Is that right, Juliet? Did you go down to Shanty Town *alone?*"

"Well, yes, I did, Daddy, but—"

"That was wrong, Juliet. And you know better than that. I'm very disappointed in you."

Juliet could take criticism from almost anyone except her father. She had been that way since she was a very small child. She always wanted to please him. And when she failed to do so, it almost broke her heart.

"I just didn't think it would be wrong, Daddy . . ."

"I believe you *did* know it was wrong, Juliet," Mrs. Jones said. "You knew good and well that we would never give you permission to go down there! So you didn't ask."

"She's off on solving another *case,* that's what," Joe said. "She's going to find out about Butcher Knife Annie. She thinks she's some kind of a criminal, and she's going to get a reward for turning her in to the police."

"We'll talk about all this later!" Mr. Jones said sharply. "And, Joe, did you talk to Juliet about this? When you see one of the Lord's children doing something wrong, you go to that person *first*. No one likes a tattletale."

Joe ducked his head and began to fill his mouth with mashed potatoes. The table was silent for the rest of the meal.

As soon as everyone had finished eating, Mr. Jones said, "Juliet, go up to your room. Your mother and I will be up to talk to you."

Juliet's heart sank again, but she knew there was no way to avoid what was coming. She went upstairs, where she sat and stared at her desk. She felt terrible. "Why did I do it?" she moaned. "I knew better than that. Why do I do things that I *know* Mom and Dad won't like?"

Shortly her parents came in. Both of them sat on Juliet's bed. "Now," her dad said, "tell me everything about this—and I mean everything."

"Well, Dad, you know the sermon this morning at church?"

"Yes. I heard the sermon. What about it?"

"Well, Brother Prince says that we're supposed to help people that are in need. Isn't that right?"

"Of course, that's right. But that doesn't mean you go down to Shanty Town by yourself."

"I know. I was wrong to do that, and I'm sorry, and I promise never to do it again. And I'll ask Jesus to forgive me, too."

"Well, that's a beginning," her mother said. "We just don't think you know how dangerous it is for a girl to go into places like that. It's bad enough just going around town by yourself. But some places are more dangerous than others. And unfortunately, Shanty Town is one of them."

"How did you get so interested in Butcher Knife Annie?" Mr. Jones asked then.

"I don't know, Daddy," Juliet said. "The other kids were all making fun of her—most of them, anyway. And she looked so old and tired, and I just felt sorry for her. And I wanted to see where she lived, and . . ."

Her mother said, "We're glad that you are concerned about others, Juliet, but you're going to have to be more careful."

"I will, Mom. I told you that."

"You've got to be very cautious and use good judgment all the time," Mrs. Jones went on. "This is a dangerous world we live in. All you have to do is open the newspaper to see what bad things can happen to boys and girls."

"Your mother's right. So from now on, I want you to stay in the parts of town where there are always lots of people. And I do believe you will from now on."

"I will, Daddy. I promise."

"Well, we're glad that you're interested in people who are less fortunate than you are, Juliet. Now let's pray about all this."

The three bowed their heads, and Mr. Jones prayed that God would help Juliet to be wise in all that she did. And he prayed about Butcher Knife Annie.

When her parents had gone back downstairs, Juliet took a deep breath. "Well, that wasn't so bad," she said. "And I *was* wrong."

After talking with her mom and dad about problems, Juliet always felt much better. She was so glad she had parents who understood and were patient with her. She'd often thought, *I wonder what it would be like to have parents that didn't take time for their kids? Joe and I are lucky to have such good ones.*

Then, suddenly, Juliet remembered. She had not told them about the picture. "Well, I'm going to take it back . . ."

But then she remembered something else. She *couldn't* take it back. She had promised she wouldn't go back into Shanty Town.

For a moment Juliet felt confused, but then she said, "Well, I'll think of something. Lord, please, You'll just have to help me. I want to be helpful to Annie, but I don't even know how to begin. You said to bring our troubles to You—and this whole thing has gotten to be a real load. So, Lord, I'm asking You to help me carry it and show me what to do."

9

Butcher
Knife Annie

Juliet enjoyed doing schoolwork. She even enjoyed helping Joe with his math. He was very good at some things, but he had trouble with sentence problems. They were so simple to Juliet that she could do them all day long. Joe did well with numbers, but somehow when a problem got put into words, he floundered around.

She'd been helping him with a hard one, when she suddenly said, "You know, Joe, we fuss at each other a lot, but I really think you're the best brother a girl ever had."

Joe stared at her. Then he flushed beet red. He ducked his head and finally mumbled, "Well, you're not so bad yourself." Coming from Joe Jones, that was like getting a medal!

Juliet punched him on the shoulder. "Tell you what. I've got some money saved up. Why don't we ask Mom if we can go and get a mini pizza for lunch? Treat's on me."

"Hey, that sounds great!"

The lunch at Pizza Hut worked out fine. She and Joe had a good time. On the way, they'd stopped at the newsstand, and Joe bought an issue of *Popular Mechanics*. He liked that magazine because he liked to invent things.

While they ate their pizzas, Joe showed her the newest spaceship that had just been launched off the pad. Right now it was circling somewhere above the earth.

After lunch Joe decided to go over and see Chili Williams and Flash Gordon. The boys were building a clubhouse. He grinned at Juliet and said, "No girls allowed in this club. You'll have to build your own clubhouse just for girls."

"We don't need a clubhouse. We've got Delores's attic. That's warmer than your place, I bet. And bigger."

Juliet strolled down to the variety store. As usual, she walked the aisles, just looking at stuff. But she didn't see anything she needed, so she left the store.

And halfway down the block she saw Butcher Knife Annie coming, bundled up in an old army overcoat.

As usual, Annie was pulling her red wagon. It was almost empty today. And the wagon tongue must have broken off. She was pulling the little wagon with a piece of heavy string.

Juliet stopped right in front of her. She smiled as nicely as she could and said, "Hello, Annie. How are you today?"

Annie stared at her with a strange look in her eye. She seemed about to say something, but then she closed her mouth like a steel trap. Without a word, she turned and hobbled off in the opposite direction.

Not knowing exactly what to do, Juliet stood and watched her disappear. She asked the Lord for help to know what to do. And then she thought, *She's headed for the park. I'll bet I can find her there.*

She stood where she was a moment longer. "I'll get something to feed the ducks. That's what I'll do," she said out loud. "And maybe I'll get something for Annie to eat, too. Something that's not out of a dumpster."

Juliet dashed into Simms Grocery Store. "Please, Mr. Simms, have you got any old bread that you're going to throw away? I need some to feed the ducks."

"That I have. And you and the ducks can have it for nothing." Mr. Simms was a tall, balding man with a pair of merry brown eyes. "You going into competition with Butcher Knife Annie?"

"Maybe you could say that. She likes to feed the ducks. I know that."

"I don't see how she feeds herself."

Juliet looked around the store and saw that

there was a sale on oranges today. A whole bag of them for a dollar. She picked up a bag and quickly took a wrinkled dollar bill from her pocket. It was the last money she had. She said, "I don't have money for tax, though."

"Oh, that's all right. I'll take care of it this time." Mr. Simms grinned. "These oranges came all the way from California. They ought to be good."

"Thank you, Mr. Simms." Juliet put the bag of oranges under one arm and the sack of stale bread under the other. She went out of the store, turned left, and headed for Elm Street. Elm Street led to the park.

Sure enough, when Juliet reached the park, she saw that Annie was already seated on the bench. A flock of ducks was crowded around her.

Juliet's heart began to beat a little faster. She had never gotten one word out of Annie and was beginning to get a little discouraged. But she went up to the old woman and said, "Hello, Annie. Can I sit beside you on the bench?"

Annie turned her head to look at Juliet. She did not say yes. But she did not say no, either. Then she reached down into her sack and took out a slice of bread. She broke it into small pieces. The ducks crowded around, quacking and shoving one another. They had no fear of her at all. They wanted to eat.

Juliet took her seat and brought out her

own bread. She tore open the plastic from one loaf and said, "Here, ducky!" She began to toss chunks of bread on the ground. She knew that Annie was watching, but Juliet did not say anything more to her. *Better to let her get used to me,* she thought.

As she sat there feeding the ducks, which seemed to come from everywhere, Juliet thought of the picture. She glanced at Annie and tried to see some resemblance. But the woman in the picture had been very young. Beside that, Annie's hat was pulled down over her face, and her face was none too clean.

Then the big Muscovy duck waddled up, and Juliet fed him piece after piece of bread. "I like this duck the best, Annie," she said. She knew she had to get some kind of conversation going. "He's so big and fat and ugly."

Annie looked at Juliet again but said absolutely nothing.

Juliet decided not to let this bother her. She continued to feed the ducks and kept on talking brightly. She knew that it was going to take time to win Annie's confidence. She talked about the ducks and how pretty they were. "It's real nice of you to feed the ducks," she said. "I'll bet they get hungry in the wintertime."

Annie did not answer, but this time Juliet saw her nod her head.

Well, that's something! she thought. *At least*

she's nodding. She continued to talk about the ducks and the pond and the weather. Finally Juliet said, "Annie, I know we don't know each other, but I've got a present for you." She reached for the bag of oranges and held them up. "These came all the way from California. Do you like oranges?"

Butcher Knife Annie looked at the bag of large orange fruit. A strange look came into her eyes. And then, for the first time, she spoke. She said, "Yes."

When Juliet pushed the bag toward her, Annie took it and placed it on her lap. Her hands stroked the oranges.

And somehow Juliet knew she had done all she could do today. "I hope you like them, Annie." She smiled as broadly as she could, nodded, and got up. She had not gone very far when she realized she was still holding two loaves of bread, not even opened. She went back. "Here," she said. "I've got to go, but these are for the ducks."

Annie took the bread, and then a surprising thing happened. Dirty as her face was and as ragged as her clothes were, a change came over her. She looked straight at Juliet, and her eyes grew brighter. Her lips suddenly turned upward in a slight smile. It was a very small smile, but it was a smile! Butcher Knife Annie said, "Thanks." Then she turned away and began to feed the ducks again.

10

A Giant Step

The Monopoly game had been going on for a long time. Joe and all of Juliet's best friends from their home school group were gathered about the board—Jenny, Flash Gordon, Chili Williams, and both Samuel and Delores Del Rio. Everybody was sprawled on the floor of the Jones living room, and a great deal of hollering and laughing was going on.

Juliet was always good at Monopoly. She knew which property to buy and when to build houses on it. Usually she won, but she had had bad luck during this game. Joe—who played Monopoly recklessly, as he did everything else—was the big winner. Now Juliet saw that she was coming toward Boardwalk, and Joe had a hotel on it.

Chili Williams said, "You'd better not land on that, Juliet. That wouldn't be smart at all."

"That's right," Flash warned, too. "You'll be out for good."

But Joe grinned broadly. "Go on. Let's see what you're going to do."

Juliet tossed the dice on the board and saw that she had rolled four.

"*Yowee!* Right in the middle of Boardwalk. You owe me two thousand dollars."

Juliet laughed. "I haven't got two *hundred* dollars. It looks like I'm out of this game."

"Too Smart Jones bites the dust!" Chili yelled.

"Don't call me that!"

"I don't see why. It's just a nickname. You call me Chili all the time."

"Well, that makes sense because you eat chili. You like chili better than anything."

"Don't you like being too smart?" Chili asked.

"I'm not too smart!" Juliet protested. She hated her nickname, but it seemed she was stuck with it. "Just call me Juliet," she begged.

"I'll tell you what, Miss Juliet Jones," Joe said. "Since you're out of the game anyhow, why don't you go fix us some more popcorn?"

"We're all out of popcorn."

"Well, fix us some peanut butter and crackers then," he said. "I'm starved."

"You can't be starved. You ate enough popcorn to fill an elephant," Flash said. "Come on. Let's see who's going to win this game."

Juliet went into the kitchen where her mother was sitting, peeling potatoes. "They want something else to eat. At least, Joe does."

Mrs. Jones looked up at her and smiled. "They're a noisy bunch, aren't they?"

"Yes, but it's fun. Can I fix some peanut butter on Ritz crackers?"

"Sure. If there's any peanut better left. Joe eats it faster than I can buy it."

Juliet began to spread peanut butter on some crackers. "This crunchy's hard to put on. It breaks the crackers," she said. She continued to spread peanut butter, and then she said, "Mom, do you know what I did yesterday?"

"What?"

"I saw Butcher Knife Annie at the park. She was feeding the ducks. And Mr. Simms gave me some stale bread, and I bought a bag of oranges with my last dollar."

"What did you do with them?"

"I fed a lot of the bread to the ducks, and I gave the oranges to Annie."

"Did she say anything?"

Juliet carefully layered another Ritz cracker with chunky peanut butter and placed it down on the plate. "She just said two words. When I asked her if she liked oranges, she said. 'Yes.' And when I left, she said, 'Thanks.'"

"Well, that's encouraging." Her mother smiled.

"I talked my head off to make conversation, Mom. I feel so sorry for her. She looked cold out there, and that shack she lives in—it's terrible. I bet she doesn't have money to buy wood for her stove. She'll get awfully cold when it gets snowy."

"There are a lot of people in the world who are not as fortunate as we are, Juliet."

"I know. When I hear about people going hungry in China or in Russia, it's just hard for me to imagine what being hungry is like. We always have plenty to eat."

"God's been good to us, and I'm grateful to Him every day," her mother said quietly.

"So am I."

"And I'm proud of the way you're trying to help Annie, Juliet. It sounds like she needs all the help she can get."

"Well, I haven't done much yet but just give her some oranges. But maybe the Lord will make me wise and show me something else I can do."

"I'm sure He will if He has something more for you to do for her."

Juliet finished putting peanut butter on enough crackers to cover the plate. She took it back into the living room, and everyone snatched at them.

But Joe said, "You're not going to give us peanut butter on crackers without something to drink, are you?"

"What do you want?"

"Mr. Pibb," Joe announced.

"We don't have any."

"Oh, it doesn't matter. Just bring anything," Delores said.

Juliet went back to the kitchen and this time made a pitcher of cherry Kool-aid.

Joe grumbled, but he drank three glasses of it anyway.

After the kids all went home, Juliet spent some time at her studies. But once in a while she would pull out the picture that she had found in Butcher Knife Annie's album. She still had not figured a way to get it back into Annie's house.

As she looked at the picture again, she thought, *I guess I could have given it to her at the park. But then she'd know I took it without her permission. I'll have to find some other way.*

She tried to decide—if the picture really was of Annie—what had happened to turn such a beautiful young woman into such a terrible mess. She tried to picture Annie when she was younger and cleaner and had on nice clothes.

What in the world happened to her that's made her like this? Doesn't she have any family? Surely she has somebody. *Somewhere.*

Juliet spent part of the day working on a new jigsaw puzzle. This one was the hardest she'd ever had. But the harder they were the better she liked them.

It had a picture on both sides. Each picture was different too, and you could not be sure which piece was right side up. On one side there was a picture of the Eiffel Tower. On the other was a woman feeding ducks. She knew this much from the two pictures on the box. But it was very difficult to find the right pieces. When Juliet finally grew tired of working on her puzzle, she slipped it under her bed.

Then she went down to the kitchen. She began looking around for some food the ducks might like. *I've started to like ducks as much as Annie does*, she thought. She found some bread hidden back in the bread box and asked her mother, "Can I take this? It looks old."

"Why, it's starting to get moldy. Yes. You can have it. What are you going to do with it?"

"I'm going to feed it to the ducks."

"Well, it's very cold out there. It's supposed to snow tonight. You bundle up."

"All right, Mom. I will." And she went to get her heavy coat.

Twenty minutes later, Juliet approached the pond. She had hoped to find Annie there, but she was not. "Maybe if I wait long enough, she'll come."

The ducks came waddling out of the water toward her, and soon she was laughing and teasing them. The big Muscovy, she thought, was probably the ugliest duck in the world. She named him "Handsome."

She was so busy feeding the noisy ducks that it came as a shock when she looked around and saw Butcher Knife Annie herself standing there. Her wagon was with her, still with only a piece of string for a handle. Juliet thought she looked tired.

"Sit down, Annie," she said. "I brought some more bread for the ducks."

Annie looked at her, then sat wearily on the bench.

Again Juliet talked about the ducks and about the weather. She thought the old woman seemed more at ease than she had before. When the bread was gone, Juliet sat back and just watched the ducks. They would stick their heads underwater and wave their bottoms in the air. It made her laugh.

She was surprised when she turned her head and saw that Annie was smiling, too. It was not a big smile, but it was more than Juliet had expected.

Suddenly Annie muttered, "I liked the oranges. I ate three of them."

"I'm so glad! I don't guess you know my name. It's Juliet. Juliet Jones."

The old woman was still for a little while. It was as if she was trying to think of a word she had not heard for a long time. Finally she said clearly, "My name is Annie Owens."

Juliet's heart leaped. *Now I've got a name!* she thought. *Annie Owens. If you know some-*

body's name, you can sometimes find where they came from. Her mind began to work.

"The oranges were real good. I hadn't had any in a long time."

"I'm glad you liked them, Annie. Are they your favorite fruit?"

Juliet talked on, and Annie answered one question out of four, perhaps. Juliet, however, did not let the conversation stop. She tried to find out as much as she could about Annie— how long she had lived here and where she had lived before she'd come to Oakwood. But Annie was not very good at talking.

Then Juliet said, "I see you broke the tongue on your wagon."

"Yes. It broke."

"You know what—I bet we could fix it. My brother, Joe, is real good at fixing things. Why don't you let me take it home with me? I'll get him to fix it. Or maybe you'd want to come, too, and meet my parents."

Annie looked startled at this and a little frightened. "No," she said. "No." She got to her feet and started off, pulling the red wagon by its string. She didn't even say good-bye.

"Good-bye, Annie," Juliet called after her. "I'll see you tomorrow. I'll bring more bread for the ducks." Juliet really did not expect Annie to pay any attention to this.

But, to her surprise, the old woman turned around. She looked very pitiful as she stood looking back at Juliet. Then, suddenly, she smiled again. "All right," she said. She hesitated a moment. "I'm glad you like ducks. I like ducks. Most people don't care for them."

"Oh, I like ducks a lot."

Juliet got up and walked to where Annie stood. She started another conversation about ducks. She found out that the old woman had named them all.

Annie looked sad when she said, "Sometimes I don't find anything to feed them. I worry about them then."

"I'll tell you what I'll do," Juliet said. "I'll go around to all of our neighbors. I'll get all the old bread and things that ducks like. And together you and I will see that they have enough to eat."

Annie looked surprised. "Most people don't care about ducks," she repeated.

"I do. I think they're cute. And I'll have my brother make a tongue for your wagon, and we'll put it on tomorrow. And I'll meet you here—just like today."

Annie didn't answer for a long time. Then she said, "That would be nice." She turned and slowly walked away, pulling the wagon.

Juliet could not wait to get home. She burst into the kitchen and excitedly told her mother all that had happened.

Joe sat at the table, listening and shaking his head. "I think she's totally weird." Then he got up. "I've got something to do in my room."

Mrs. Jones said, "I'm glad you've made a friend of Annie, Juliet."

"I told her I'd get Joe to fix the tongue to her wagon. She has to pull it with a string."

"I'll bet he could do that. Why don't you go up and ask him?"

"All right. I will."

Juliet bounded up the stairs. "Joe, Annie's wagon is broken. Will you help fix it?"

"What's wrong with it?"

"The tongue came off. And she doesn't know how to fix it. And I don't know how to make a new one, either. But I bet you could do it. You're so smart with tools and fixing things."

Joe suddenly looked ashamed. "Aw, I'm sorry I said what I did about her. I'm getting to be an old grump. OK. Let's go down to Dad's shop. We'll make her the best wagon tongue you ever saw."

11

Butcher Knife Annie's Story

Juliet and Jenny met in front of the ice cream shop. It was very cold, and both were heavily bundled up.

"Look what I've got, Jenny."

Jenny frowned at the piece of wood that Juliet held in her hands. "What's that?" she asked.

"It's a new handle for Annie's wagon. The old one broke, and she has to pull it with a string."

"Did you make it?"

"No. Joe did. I'm not sure I can put it on right, but I'm going to try."

"Are you going now?"

"Yes. I told her I'd meet her down at the pond. I'm going to stop and get some old bread from Mr. Simms if he has any. To feed the ducks. Why don't you come with me?"

Jenny frowned a little, but finally she nodded. "All right, but I still don't think it's a good idea."

They stopped at the little grocery store, and Mr. Simms gave them four loaves of bread. "It's about a week old," he told Juliet. "But I don't guess the ducks will mind."

"I don't think they will. Thank you very much, Mr. Simms."

The two girls walked on to the city park. "Look," Juliet said, "Annie's already there."

Jenny's face grew a little pale. "I think I'll stay back here. That way I can run for help if I need to."

"Don't be silly! She's very nice. She really is. She's just old and tired."

Juliet did not try to argue, however. She just took the bag of bread Jenny had been carrying and walked to where Annie was sitting on the park bench. She put down the sack and said, "Hello, Annie. Look what I've got. A new tongue for your wagon. Here, let me see if I can put it on. My brother showed me how."

Juliet was not very good with tools, but she managed to get the wagon tongue in place. Then she stood up, pleased with herself. "Now you won't have to pull it with a string."

"That's very nice," Annie said. She sat looking at the wagon. Then she said, "Thank you, Juliet."

"Why, you're welcome. Look, I brought some bread too."

Juliet gave Annie one of the loaves, and she opened another. As usual, the ducks came waddling and quacking toward them. Handsome was in the lead, and Juliet laughed. "You're the greediest duck in the world—and the ugliest!"

"I don't think he's ugly," Annie said.

"Don't you?"

"He's just different from the others."

They sat together on the bench, talking about the ducks. Juliet noticed that Jenny kept edging closer all the time they were talking. Annie seemed not to see her, not even when Jenny stood only a few feet away.

"Annie, why did you move to Oakwood?"

For a long time it was quiet. Juliet did not think she was going to answer.

And then Butcher Knife Annie began to talk. She spoke slowly and paused between sentences. "My husband died four years ago. We lived in a town sixty miles away." Annie tore a piece of bread and scattered crumbs on the ground. After a time she said, "We owed some back taxes, and I tried to work to pay all of them. But I didn't have enough. They took my house, and I didn't have anything left. I thought I'd do better in a place like Oakwood, but . . ."

"Do you have any family, Annie?"

"I've got one sister."

"What's her name?"

"Her name is Sally Owens-Bright."

"Does she live in the town where you did?"

"No. She lives in Decatur, Texas."

"Didn't you write her and tell her you were in trouble?"

"No. I never did. I didn't want to burden her with my problems." Annie shook her head and looked at the ground. "We were raised not to ask for help from other people."

Juliet thought about that. "But all of us need help *sometimes* . . ."

"Well, that's not the way my parents taught us. But then I got sick and haven't been able to work."

Jenny was edging still closer.

Just as Juliet was about to ask another question, Annie looked up and saw the other girl standing there. She jumped. Then she got up quickly, looking very disturbed. She grabbed the handle of the wagon and started off.

"Wait, Annie!" Juliet cried.

But Annie paid no attention.

Juliet turned to Jenny. "Look what you did!" she scolded. "You scared her!"

"I didn't do anything," Jenny said. "I just wanted to hear what you were talking about."

Juliet was upset, but she knew it wasn't Jenny's fault. "Did you hear what she said?"

"I heard some. She's got a sister in Decatur, Texas."

"Where is that, I wonder? Texas is a big state."

"I don't know. But we can go to my house and look in our map book."

Soon the two girls were at the Whites' kitchen table, staring down at a map of Texas. They had found the name Decatur in the index. Juliet said, "It's I-4. I'll find the 4, and you find the I."

"All right," Jenny agreed.

The girls moved their fingers down and across the map until Juliet said, "There it is. Right there. Right up over Dallas."

"That's a long way from here. It doesn't look like a very big place."

"It's not big, and we know her sister's name. Sally Owens-Bright." Juliet felt pleased. "Now we have two clues. I always feel good when I get a clue like this. I think the Lord gave it to us."

"Well, you've worked hard enough at it," Jenny said. "You've got a kind heart, Juliet Jones. Maybe I ought to call you Too Kind Jones."

Juliet suddenly laughed. "No. Just Juliet. That's all I want to be called."

12

The New
Annie

The school day passed slowly for Juliet. She had her mind on the case of Butcher Knife Annie instead of on her studies. And as always when she was trying to solve a mystery, she grew a little snappish.

"I wish you would get with it!" Joe finally yelled at her. "We've got to finish this work. I want to go out and play ball."

Juliet wanted to snap back. But she knew that she had been dragging her feet. "I'm sorry, Joe," she said. "Come on. I'll help you do your problems."

After schoolwork and chores were done, Joe went off to play ball.

Juliet was sitting in her room, thinking about Butcher Knife Annie, when a knock came at her door. "Come," she said. She was surprised when both of her parents came in. She said at once, "What have I done wrong now?"

Mr. Jones laughed. "You don't have to have done anything wrong for us to come to your room."

"You haven't done anything wrong, Juliet. But your father and I have been talking about Annie. We've decided we ought to do something to help her."

"Oh, that would be wonderful! I don't really know what to do next. All I know is what I told you—that she has a sister in Decatur, Texas. And her sister's name is Sally Owens-Bright."

"Juliet, I think it's reached the point where your mother and I need to talk to Annie."

"But she's afraid of people, Dad!"

"Well, we've been praying for her. And we think it's time she learns to trust somebody," her mother said.

"Your mother and I have both been very impressed with how you've cared about what happens to Annie. And we've started caring, too."

"That's the way it is sometimes, Juliet," Mrs. Jones said. "When you see somebody else caring, *you* start to care."

"Do you really think we can help her?" Juliet asked.

"I don't think the Lord would put her on all our hearts if He didn't have some plan. Let's go talk to her."

"She's always at the pond about this time—feeding the ducks."

"Well," her dad said, "we'll go feed some ducks, too."

The Joneses went first to Simms Grocery Store.

"I'm all out of stale bread," Mr. Simms said. "Sorry about that, Mr. Jones."

"Well, give us some fresh bread, then. We'll give the ducks a real treat today."

They left the store with three loaves of bread and made their way to the park.

Juliet was nervous. As soon as they got near the pond, she grew even more nervous. "There she is. But when she sees you, she's going to run away. I know she will. That's what she did when she saw Jenny."

"Then let's just pray right now that she won't."

The three bowed their heads and prayed for Annie. Then Mr. Jones said, "All right. Here we go."

They walked toward the pond.

Annie looked up and saw them coming. Her face got a worried look.

Juliet thought, *She's used to me, but this time I have two grown-ups with me. She's scared.*

"Annie, these are my parents," Juliet called quickly before Annie could get up. "Mom and Dad, this is Annie." She was glad that she'd warned her parents that the woman would be very nervous.

Her father said quietly, "We just thought we'd come down and feed the ducks today."

Perhaps that made Annie feel better. "You like ducks?" she asked.

"Oh yes. We always had ducks on our farm. Ducks like that big one there."

"That's Handsome," Juliet said.

"Well, he's a Muscovy duck, and we had a whole flock of them when I was a boy. I had to get out every day and gather their eggs."

"I did the same thing when I was a girl," Annie said. "I love Muscovy eggs."

"So did I. They're better than hen eggs. Don't you think so, Rachel?"

Mrs. Jones smiled at Annie. "I haven't ever eaten one. I don't know whether I'd like them or not."

"Oh, you'd like them," Annie said.

Juliet could tell that Butcher Knife Annie was feeling more comfortable now. Juliet was proud of her parents. They had spoken quietly, and they had won Annie's confidence very quickly.

When half the bread was gone, Mr. Jones said, "Maybe we ought to save some of this for tomorrow. They'll be hungry for more then."

Annie looked out at the pond. "I know how they feel. When you live from day to day, you're not quite sure how much to save for the next day."

Juliet saw her parents exchange a quick glance. She knew they were both very caring people. They felt sorry for this old woman.

"Juliet tells me you lost your husband, Annie."

"Yes. He was such a good man. But he made some bad decisions with his money."

"That happens to the best of men," Mr. Jones said.

"I know. And I never blamed him for it. But it bothered me to owe people money. I was always taught to pay back what I owe. And I worked for a long time trying to pay all of our debts."

"That was a wonderful thing for you to do, Annie," Mrs. Jones said. "Did you get everything paid off?"

"Yes, I did, but it took a long time."

Suddenly Juliet knew it was time to make a confession to Annie. She swallowed hard and then reached into her pocket. She pulled out the picture.

"Annie, last week I was over at your house. And the door was open. And your picture album was right there. And I have to tell you I looked in it. It was awful of me, and I shouldn't have done it, and I'm sorry. But the door was open and . . . I shut it before I left."

"It blows open like that a lot."

"This picture was in the back. There were two just alike. I took this one because I thought

107

it might help me find out who you were. I didn't want to keep it. I thought maybe I could find somebody to help you . . ."

Annie took the picture with a hand that trembled. "That's my husband, Carl," she said. "And that's me. It's an old picture."

"He was a very handsome man," Mrs. Jones said gently.

"Yes, he was."

"And you were a very beautiful young lady."

"Not anymore, though."

"Tell us about you and Carl," Mr. Jones urged.

"Well, we had a good life together. It was just hard for me to go out and work to pay back the money. I never blamed Carl, though. It wasn't his fault. He put our money into a company that failed. He couldn't know that would happen."

Butcher Knife Annie talked longer than Juliet had ever heard her talk before. Then she said, "And I was ashamed to stay in the town where we had all those debts. Even though I paid them all off, I was embarrassed. So I came down here to start a new life. I thought I'd find a job. I couldn't. And I got sick, and I was ashamed to ask anyone for help . . ."

"I think we can do something about that," Mr. Jones said. He smiled and added, "There's always a job somewhere for someone who wants to work and is able to."

"It's getting cold out here," Mrs. Jones said suddenly. "Annie, I wish you'd come home with us and get warm."

"Oh no. I couldn't do that."

"Oh, please come, Annie! I'll show you my room—and all my stuffed animals."

"Do you have stuffed animals? I used to collect stuffed animals."

Juliet and her parents finally convinced Annie to come home with them. They made their way slowly back through the park, Annie pulling the red wagon. It took a long time to walk to the Jones house. By the time they got there, Juliet was sure everybody was as hungry as she was.

Juliet's dad drew her mom aside and said, "You take care of Annie. She's in pretty bad shape. I'll do a little detective work." He winked at Juliet, who was listening. "You're not the only detective in this family, Juliet Jones."

What happened next Juliet would always remember. It took a little persuasion, but Mrs. Jones convinced Annie to go upstairs with her and take a bath. "I've got so many clothes that I've outgrown, Annie. But they should be just right for you."

Annie looked a little frightened, but she allowed Juliet's mother to lead her away.

As they went upstairs, Juliet followed her dad into his study. He got on the phone. She heard him say, "Yes, we're trying to locate a woman named Sally Owens-Bright. Yes. She's somewhere in Decatur, Texas." He waited a moment and then said, "Good. I'll call back in half an hour."

When Juliet's mother came back downstairs, she and Juliet put together a nice lunch. There was some pot roast that was left over from the night before. It filled the kitchen and the dining area with a delightful smell. There was fresh bread, and Juliet warmed up some golden corn and a bowl of green peas. They had just put everything on the table when Juliet heard footsteps on the stairs.

Both Juliet and her mom went to the hall and looked up.

"Why, Annie, you look beautiful!"

Butcher Knife Annie was, indeed, transformed!

She had on a pretty blue dress that Mrs. Jones had once been very proud of. Her hair had been washed and was a beautiful shade of gray. And she was smiling shyly.

Juliet took her hand. "You look beautiful, Annie," she repeated.

"It feels so good. There's no way to take a bath out where I live. And I've missed that so much."

"We're going to do something about all that. But come along. Right now we're going to eat," Mrs. Jones said.

They sat down at the table, and Juliet's father asked God's blessing on the food. He also asked a special blessing on their guest.

At first, Annie was timid and had to be urged to eat. But soon she was eating hungrily.

All at once, Joe, who had been staring at her, asked in his blunt way, "Miss Annie, why do you carry that butcher knife?"

"Well, I was just afraid that someone would hurt me. I guess it doesn't look very good. But it does keep people away."

"It does that all right," Juliet said. "But I don't think you need to carry it."

"I guess I don't. Nobody's bothered me the whole time I've lived here."

At that moment the phone rang.

"I'll get it," Mr. Jones said, and he left the table. He was gone for some time. When he came back, he was smiling. "We found her!"

"Found who, Dad?" Juliet asked.

"We found Sally Owens-Bright. She lives just outside of Decatur. And I've talked with your sister, Annie. She wants to see you. As a matter of fact, she wants us to take you there. She wants you to live with her."

"Why, she can't take care of me!"

Mr. Jones sat down again. "I think you're wrong there. Your sister and her husband have a big farm. They grow cotton—and that's good cotton country. Besides, they've been looking for you, Annie. Did you know that?"

"No. We lost touch a long time ago. Do they really *want* me to come?"

"They really want you. So tomorrow we'll all get in our van, and we'll take a trip to Texas."

Annie suddenly began to cry. Tears ran down her cheeks. She said, "The Lord be praised! He's been so good to me to give me a family."

"There's a Bible verse about that," Juliet said. "It says that God can set the solitary in families."

Her mom smiled. "You always know a verse for everything, don't you?"

Joe said, "Wow! We're going to Texas? Maybe I'll see some cowboys."

"You mean Dallas Cowboys, the football players?" Juliet teased.

"No. I mean cowboys on horses."

"This will be a homecoming for you, Annie. And there won't be anyone there who will call you Butcher Knife Annie."

Annie Owens looked around at the happy faces. "I guess the Lord brought me to this place." Her eyes came to rest on Juliet. "And He brought you to me. You're such a determined girl, Juliet. The way I treated you, most girls would have run away scared."

Juliet felt pleased. "I just thought the Lord wanted me to help," she said. "Besides, there was a mystery. And I do dearly love a mystery!"